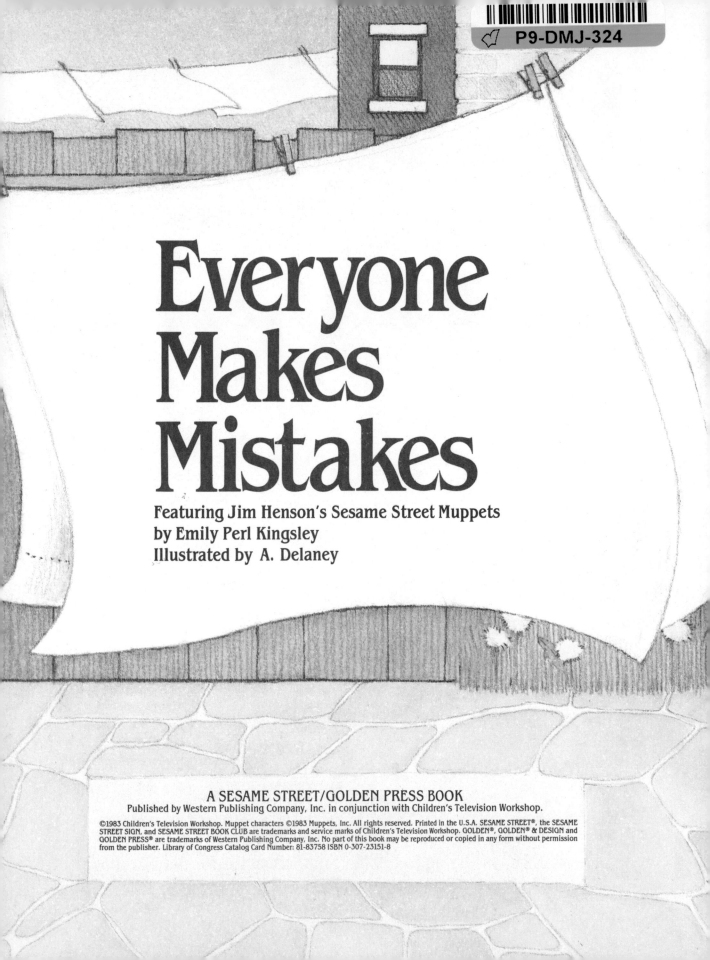

Everyone Makes Mistakes

Featuring Jim Henson's Sesame Street Muppets
by Emily Perl Kingsley
Illustrated by A. Delaney

A SESAME STREET/GOLDEN PRESS BOOK
Published by Western Publishing Company, Inc. in conjunction with Children's Television Workshop.

One day Big Bird was walking along thinking about what he was going to get Mr. Snuffle-upagus for his birthday, when–WHAP!–something cold and wet hit him in the face.

Big Bird had walked right into Susan's fresh clean clothes
that she had washed and hung out in the sun to dry and
knocked the clothesline down. Wet socks and jeans and
towels and sheets fell to the ground.

"Oh, no! Susan will be so angry with me when she sees her clean laundry all dirty on the ground," said Big Bird. "What will I tell her?

"Hmm. I could tell Susan that a big flock of birds
was flying south for the winter and flew right into
the laundry hanging on the line and pulled it all down.
"No, that's no good," he said. "Birds fly south
in the fall and it's spring now."

Big Bird thought and thought. "I know," he said. "I could tell Susan that Biff and Sully drove their big crane through here on their way to the construction site at the corner, and ran right into her nice clean laundry!

"No, that's no good. Biff and Sully wouldn't drive their crane through a yard. They would drive it right down Sesame Street to the construction site."

"Let's see," said Big Bird. "I could tell Susan that a giraffe escaped from the zoo and ran straight through the yard and got all tangled up in her laundry and scattered it all over. I could tell her that."

Big Bird thought for a moment. "No. Susan would never believe a silly story about a giraffe escaping from the zoo."

"Maybe I could tell Susan that today was the day of the
Great Sesame Street Bicycle Race! I could tell her that the
racers rode their bikes straight into her laundry and dragged
it on the ground!

"Nah. The Great Bicycle Race was last week. Susan will remember it because she won the race.

"I can't tell her that."

"Well," Big Bird said, "I could say that there was a big
fire on Sesame Street. All the fire engines came racing
through here on their way to put out the fire and the ladders
and hoses got caught on the clothesline and pulled it down.

"No, I can't tell Susan that," he said sadly. "She would
know there wasn't a fire on Sesame Street today."

"I've got it!" said Big Bird. "Alphabet Bates came down
in his parachute to deliver a letter, and he landed right on
Susan's clothesline!

"On second thought, I'd better not say that either. I can't blame my mistake on Alphabet Bates."

"How about a circus? That's it! The circus came to
perform right here on Sesame Street and the tightrope
walker practiced her act on Susan's clothesline,
and knocked down the clothes.

"Wait a minute. That's a terrible idea. A circus act here in Susan's backyard? I can't tell her that's what happened."

"There could have been a rodeo here today.
Rodeo Rosie and her friends were roping steers here.
What if I tell her that?

"No," Big Bird said. "That story is just
as silly as the others."

"I know! A tornado might have hit Sesame Street!
It certainly looks like a tornado came through here."

Big Bird sighed. "No, I can't do that. I can't tell Susan
something that didn't happen. That would be wrong.
"Oh, no! Here she comes now!"

"What happened, Big Bird?" cried Susan, when she saw the mess. "Look at my clean laundry all over the ground!"

"Well...it's like this," stammered Big Bird. "A flock of... no, I mean Biff and Sully, er, that is...a giraffe on a bicycle chasing a fire engine...no, I mean...Alphabet Bates

parachuted into a circus…no, Rodeo Rosie was roping
in a rodeo…or was it a tornado…?"

Big Bird stopped and shook his head.

"No, Susan, it was none of those things," he said.

"What are you trying to tell me, Big Bird?" asked Susan.

"I'm trying to tell you," said Big Bird, "that I wasn't looking where I was going and I walked right into your laundry and knocked it down."

"Oh," said Susan.

"I'm sorry, Susan," said Big Bird. "Are you angry?"

"Well," answered Susan, "a little. But I'll get over it."
"I'll help you wash the clothes again," said Big Bird.
   Big Bird and Susan began to pick up the clothes.
   "Don't worry, Big Bird," said Susan, "everyone makes mistakes."